In Good Hands

Behind the scenes at a center for orphaned and injured birds

Stephen R. Swinburne

Sierra Club Books for Children
San Francisco

To all the good hands at raptor centers everywhere
who rescue and rehabilitate birds of prey — and release
them to the wild

The Sierra Club, founded in 1892 by John Muir, has devoted itself to the study and protection of the earth's scenic and ecological resources — mountains, wetlands, woodlands, wild shores and rivers, deserts and plains. The publishing program of the Sierra Club offers books to the public as a nonprofit educational service in the hope that they may enlarge the public's understanding of the Club's basic concerns. The point of view expressed in each book, however, does not necessarily represent that of the Club. The Sierra Club has some sixty chapters in the United States and Canada. For information about how you may participate in its programs to preserve wilderness and the quality of life, please address inquiries to Sierra Club, 85 Second Street, San Francisco, CA 94105, or visit our website at www.sierraclub.org.

First Edition

Acknowledgments
The author wishes to thank the staff of the Vermont Raptor Center at the Vermont Institute of Natural Science (VINS) in Woodstock, Vermont, for their help and cooperation during this project.

In particular, the author is grateful to Michael D. Cox, director of the Raptor Center; Julie Tracy, former director of the Raptor Center; Sarah B. Laughlin, past executive director of VINS; and Steve Faccio, naturalist.

Finally, special thanks is due Hannah Regier, without whose patience, humor, and energy this book could not have been done.

Important Note
Raptors are protected by law and may not be handled without proper permits and training.

Library of Congress Cataloging-in-Publication Data
Swinburne, Stephen R.
     In good hands : behind the scenes at a center for orphaned and injured birds / Stephen R. Swinburne. — 1st ed.
        p.   cm.
     Includes index.
     Summary: Provides a behind-the-scenes look at the Vermont Raptor Center, a facility where volunteers rescue and rehabilitate hurt or abandoned birds of prey and eventually release them back into the wild.
     ISBN 0-87156-397-5
     1. Birds of prey — Wounds and injuries — Treatment — Vermont — Juvenile literature. 2. Birds of prey — Vermont — Juvenile literature. 3. Wildlife rehabilitation — Vermont — Juvenile literature. 4. Wildlife rescue — Vermont — Juvenile literature. 5. Vermont Raptor Center — Juvenile literature. [1.Birds of prey — Wounds and injuries — Treatment. 2. Birds of prey. 3. Wildlife rescue. 4. Vermont Raptor Center.] I. Title.
SF994.5.S95   1998
639.9'789 — dc21   97-19325

Book and jacket design: Bonnie Smetts
Illustrations: Rik Olson
Printed in Singapore

10 9 8 7 6 5 4 3 2 1

Contents

CHAPTER 1

Rescued!

Luckily, rescue was at hand for the downy little barred owl.

Early one summer morning, Hannah peeked around a boulder at a baby barred owl huddled against the stump of a pine tree. The owl was small, with brown eyes like dark chocolate.

"Poor baby," thought Hannah. "But at least it doesn't seem to be hurt."

The bird's nesting tree had been cut down by loggers. Hannah had waited and watched for a while to be certain the parent owls wouldn't be coming back to care for their baby. She knew that, most times, birds on the ground have just left the nest and are still being fed by the parents. But this time, the baby really was an orphan.

She walked toward the small creature. The owl clacked its bill and kicked with feet that stuck out from its body like skis. Gently but firmly, Hannah picked it up.

The owl was in good hands. Sixteen-year-old Hannah Regier, a volunteer at the Vermont Raptor Center, was trained to rescue and care for raptors. She also had a special love for these wild and powerful birds of prey. Hawks and owls, falcons and eagles, vultures and kites — they

are the hunters of the bird world. They fly in lazy circles high in the summer sky and glide silently through forests on a moonlit winter's night, always on the alert for prey. They can spot a mouse in the grass from more than a hundred feet away and can hear an almost silent rustle in the leaves. Raptors fly swiftly and strike suddenly with hooked beaks and sharp, powerful talons.

But the bird Hannah had just picked up was still a baby, and it wasn't nearly ready to be a hunter yet. Hannah hurried to the waiting Raptor Center station wagon. She carefully nestled the baby barred owl in a warm, dark box. As a fellow volunteer drove back to the Raptor Center, Hannah peeked in at the round ball of gray and white down.

"This little guy looks so alone and scared," she said aloud. She felt sad to think that the young bird was separated from its parents forever.

But she was glad the loggers had called the Center about the destroyed nest. Now, she hoped, the little owl would have a chance to grow up.

This owl was one of the almost 600 birds of prey brought into the Vermont Raptor Center every year. There are other rescue centers like this one all across the country. They care for birds of prey that have been hurt or abandoned or have lost their homes. Birds that are orphans, like the baby barred owl, have had their nests destroyed or have been blown out of them by storms. The parents may not have been able to rescue their young, or they may have been killed.

Birds of prey are also taken to the Center to be treated for all sorts of injuries. Cars are the number-one cause of injury, especially for hawks and owls, which like to hunt along open clearings beside highways. They often get hit while chasing a mouse or rabbit onto the road. Other birds of prey get hurt when they dive into a window or fence or crash into overhead wires. Some are injured by pet dogs or cats.

After a short drive, Hannah and the other volunteer arrived at the Raptor Center, a small cluster of buildings overlooking a gentle landscape of wildflower meadows, wooded hillsides, and stone walls. The volunteers drove past the display cages, where visitors can see raptors up close. They continued through a gate in a high wooden fence to the infirmary, located out of public view. When birds first arrive at the Center, they're taken here for a complete physical exam.

Hannah carried the baby owl inside and put it on a table. She and a volunteer veterinarian carefully felt the tiny bones of the outspread wings. Hannah ran a finger along the owl's breast and then gently down its back. They moved the legs and feet back and forth to be sure nothing was broken. The young owl grabbed Hannah's gloved hand with its beak. Hannah smiled.

"Hey — you're a feisty one!"

Hannah weighed the owl on a small scale. After recording its weight, she gave the owl some water. Most birds are dehydrated when they are first brought to the Raptor Center. It's important to replenish their body fluids.

Hannah and the veterinarian were satisfied that the owl was in good shape. "Now I'll bet you're hungry," Hannah said. She cut up a small, dead mouse. Then she picked up the owl and held the food near its beak. The owl lifted its head, opened its bill, and — with a blink of its eyes — swallowed the pieces whole.

The Vermont Raptor Center is nestled in a clearing at the edge of a forest.

NORTH AMERICAN RAPTORS

The 52 species of raptors found in North America fall into 6 main groups — kites, hawks, eagles, vultures, falcons, and owls.

Kites are graceful fliers that glide down to their prey (mostly insects and snails) rather than diving, as many other birds of prey do. Four species of kites are found in North America.

Of the 17 species of hawks, 12 are buteos — high fliers such as the red-tailed hawk. Three are low-flying accipiters that speed among trees as they hunt. The other 2 North American hawk-like raptors are the Northern harrier, which hunts voles in open fields and marshes, and the fish-eating osprey.

Only 2 species of eagles — the golden eagle and the bald eagle — live in North America. The majestic bald eagle is the national bird of the United States.

Vultures are the only raptors that don't catch live prey; they feed on carrion, the flesh of animals that have already died. There are 3 kinds of vultures in North America — the turkey vulture, the black vulture, and the enormous California condor, which came close to extinction and is still very rare.

Falcons include 6 species. The largest is the gyrfalcon, and the smallest is the American kestrel. The most familiar species is the sky-diving peregrine falcon. The crested caracara, the only caracara found in North America, is a relative of the falcons.

Finally, there are 19 species of owls, most of them night hunters. They range in size from the tiny elf owl, with a wingspan of about 5 inches, to the magnificent great gray owl, with a wingspan of more than 4 feet.

KITES
- Black-shouldered kite
- Mississippi kite
- American swallow-tailed kite
- Snail kite

HARRIERS
- Northern harrier

ACCIPITERS
- Sharp-shinned hawk
- Cooper's hawk
- Northern goshawk

BUTEOS
- Red-tailed hawk
- Swainson's hawk
- Rough-legged hawk
- Red-shouldered hawk
- Broad-winged hawk
- Ferruginous hawk
- Harris' hawk
- Zone-tailed hawk
- Black hawk
- Gray hawk
- Short-tailed hawk
- White-tailed hawk

OSPREYS
- Osprey

EAGLES
- Bald eagle
- Golden eagle

AMERICAN VULTURES
- Turkey vulture
- Black vulture
- California condor

CARACARAS
- Crested caracara

FALCONS
- Gyrfalcon
- Merlin
- American kestrel
- Peregrine falcon
- Prairie falcon
- Aplomado falcon

OWLS
- Barred owl
- Barn owl
- Great gray owl
- Snowy owl
- Short-eared owl
- Eastern screech owl
- Western screech owl
- Whiskered screech owl
- Long-eared owl
- Great horned owl
- Boreal owl
- Northern saw-whet owl
- Burrowing owl
- Northern hawk owl
- Spotted owl
- Flammulated owl
- Elf owl
- Ferruginous pygmy owl
- Northern pygmy owl

Would the adult barred owl become a surrogate mother to the young orphan?

Afterward, Hannah carried the infant to a large outdoor cage occupied by an adult female barred owl. She hoped the adult bird would become a surrogate, or substitute, mother.

Hannah held her breath as she placed the little owl on a platform. She knew that sometimes an adult bird will reject a younger one. The big owl flew over to inspect the young bird. For a moment, the two owls stared at each other. Then they sat side by side without moving for a long time.

It was a good beginning. Now, Hannah hoped, the adult would begin to feed and care for the orphan. She resolved to keep a close watch to see how the young owl and the adult would settle in together.

CHAPTER 2

Meet the Raptors

At feeding time, Hannah carries containers of rodents to distribute among the raptors.

Back at the public area of the Raptor Center, a full morning's work awaited Hannah. First, she had to check on all the birds in the outdoor cages. This was her favorite part of the day because it gave her a chance to talk with visitors about the raptors on display.

Of the 52 kinds of raptors found in North America, about 25 species were represented at the Raptor Center. There were bald eagles and great horned owls, peregrine falcons and red-tailed hawks.

One of Hannah's most important chores was to feed the birds and give them fresh water. She stopped first at the Cooper's hawk cage. The Cooper's hawk was Hannah's favorite; she'd named him "Coop." As she was filling his water pan, a family — a young girl and boy and their parents — came by to see the birds.

"How did these birds get here, anyway? How did they get hurt?" asked the father.

"This hawk was hit by a car, and its wing was injured," said Hannah. "The driver brought him here."

Hannah pulled on a thick leather glove and lifted Coop onto her

wrist. The hawk unfolded and stretched his left wing to its full length. His right wing, crooked, drooped at his side. His red eyes glowed.

The girl pointed to Hannah's glove. "Why are you wearing that?"

"See his talons?" Hannah said. "If I didn't wear this glove, those claws would dig right into my skin."

"Will the hawk get better?" asked the boy.

"Coop's wing broke in a way that we couldn't fix," said Hannah. "He can't fly, so he has to stay in captivity. But we take really good care of him."

Hannah explained to the family that about half of the injured birds are rehabilitated, or healed, and released back into the wild. But some never return to their natural homes because their injuries are too severe. Birds of prey depend on fast flight and quick aerial maneuvers to capture their prey. A hawk that has a broken wing wouldn't survive in the wild

The national bird of the United States, the bald eagle is a symbol of strength and power.

because it couldn't feed itself. So these birds stay at the Center, where they "help" volunteers teach visitors about birds of prey and their role in the environment.

Hannah left food for Coop and walked to the bald eagle cage. The cage was the size of a small classroom, with tree branches crisscrossed inside. The huge eagle was perched on the highest branch.

Hannah unlocked a small door on the side of the cage and stepped in. Her skin tingled and her heart beat faster as she turned around and latched the door from the inside. She knew how deadly the eagle's hooked beak and razor-sharp talons could be. Hannah looked up at the bird's stern face. The eagle glared down with its great, yellow eyes. Hannah slowly added fresh water to the eagle's pool but never took her eyes off the bird. Would the bald eagle move? she wondered. She backed away quietly and stepped out of the cage door. When she locked the door from the outside, she felt her heart calm.

Hannah heard children laughing and shook off her jittery feeling. A group from a nearby day camp was visiting. Their first stop was the eagle cage; everyone loved to ask questions about the bald eagle.

"Wow, that's awesome! Is it a boy or a girl?"

"She's a girl, and she's full-grown," said Hannah. "Male and female bald eagles look the same. Here — let me show you something amazing." She lined up three children and had them hold their arms out to the sides and touch fingertips. "That's how wide her wingspan is — 7½ feet!" Impressed, the kids stared up at the huge bird.

"Hey," said one boy, "my dad's bald! That eagle doesn't look bald to me!" The kids giggled.

EQUIPPED FOR HUNTING

Raptors are perfectly designed for hunting. They have the best long-range vision of any creature on earth. With eyes like built-in telescopes, they can see at least eight times better than people. That means that if you can spot a nickel on the ground from 20 feet, a raptor can spot it from 160 feet. In dim light, owls can see many times better than humans can.

One reason raptors see so well is because their eyes are large. If your eyes were in the same proportion to your body, they'd be as big as softballs!

Raptors' wings are also designed to help them hunt successfully. Birds such as buteo hawks, eagles, and vultures have long wings that help them soar and circle high in the air to look for prey. Others, such as accipiters and some falcons, have more rounded wings for turning quickly and zipping low among forest trees.

Owls, with their soft, fringed wing feathers, can glide toward prey in total silence.

All birds of prey have four toes on each foot. The toes have curved claws, called talons, which are razor sharp. Raptors use their feet to grasp and stab or crush their prey. If a raptor grabs a mouse, it will not let go until the prey stops moving. Feet with talons that shut tightly ensure that a precious catch won't be dropped.

Raptors have upper beaks that are hooked and pointed for tearing up prey once they have killed it. Some birds, such as falcons and owls, use their beaks to kill prey they have clutched in their talons.

"I know," said Hannah. "But with white feathers on their heads, bald eagles *look* bald from a distance. Young eagles have dark heads; the head and tail feathers turn white when they're about 5 years old."

The eagle ran up a wide branch and pumped the air with her wings. The force of the moving wings could be felt outside the cage. Awed by the power of the bird, the kids fell silent for a minute.

Then a girl asked, "Hey, how come she's in a cage? It looks like she can fly."

"I wish she could," said Hannah, "but she has a broken wing from crashing into overhead wires. We can't fix it well enough for her to fly, so she lives here."

Hannah lifted a small door in the cage and placed a dead, white rat on a feeding tray. In the wild, most bald eagles live near beaches, large rivers, or lakes and eat lots of fish. But the eagles at the Center eat mostly rats, which are easier to supply.

The eagle swooped down and opened her sharp talons; then she

Hannah stocks the eagle's feeding tray with dinner — a fat, white rat.

locked them onto the rat. The bird sprang to a wide branch in the middle of the cage. She ripped open the rat with her curved beak.

"Yuck!"

"I know — it looks gross," said Hannah, "but that's how eagles eat."

The eagle threw her head back and called, *"Kek, kek, kek!"* Her harsh cry pierced the quiet of the morning. For a moment, all the birds at the Center became very still.

Hannah moved on to check the snowy owls. Some children were watching one of the magnificent white birds preening its feathers on a log in the sun. As Hannah approached the cage, the owl froze and stared with large, golden eyes.

"Isn't he beautiful?" said Hannah. "Most snowy owls live very far from here, in the Arctic tundra. They're one of the largest and most powerful of all owls. And they're unusual because they hunt in the daytime, instead of at night like most owls. Their white feathers help camouflage them in the snow."

The children gazed at the owl. They'd never seen an owl so big or so close up.

"This is a male," said Hannah. "Look! There's the female in the back of the cage." Dark spots covered the breast of the female owl.

"How come they're here instead of in the Arctic?" asked one girl.

"Good question," said Hannah. "Snowy owls eat small rodents called lemmings, and when there aren't enough lemmings up north, the snowies fly south to hunt."

"Are these two hurt?" someone asked.

"Yes, they were shot by hunters," explained Hannah. "Their wings

The snowy owl's plumage blends into the white expanses of its Arctic home.

An owl coughs up the undigestible parts of its prey in the form of a little pellet.

Smashed open, the pellet reveals rodent fur and many tiny bones.

were so badly broken that they can't fly very far. Now, wait a second and I'll show you something."

She went into the owl cage and looked around on the ground. As she moved, the male owl's eyes followed her with their unblinking stare.

"Ah, here's one," she called. She stepped out of the cage, and the children gathered around. "Look what I found. It's an owl pellet." She showed them a small, gray clump the size of a rabbit's foot. "Owls swallow their prey whole. About 24 hours after an owl eats a mouse, it coughs up a pellet of fur and bones — the stuff it can't digest."

The pellet had dried in the sun. Hannah passed it around so the children could feel it. Then she put the pellet on a flat stone and broke it in half. Owl pellets are very clean — just dry fur and tiny bones. Hannah and the children got down on their knees and examined the pellet for bones as the owl watched silently.

"Look how he's watching us!" exclaimed one boy.

"Yeah, his eyes are amazing — as big as ours!" said Hannah.

"*Awesome!*" said one girl. "Where could we see a wild one?"

"Well, they like airport landing fields and even beaches," said Hannah. "Maybe places like that look like the Arctic tundra to them. I once saw one sitting on a sand dune. I tried getting closer, but it hooted at me — '*Hoooo, hoo, hoo, hoo!*' — and flew away."

The hoot stirred the male owl. He blinked one eye and then the other and bobbed his head from side to side. Suddenly, he hopped from his log perch and ran a few feet. He spread his giant wings and glided to a ledge at the other end of the cage without making the slightest sound.

Hannah left the children watching the snowy owls and continued with her rounds. She walked along a path beside the display cages, stopping to check on the goshawk, the red-tailed hawk, and the 10-inch American kestrel — the smallest species of falcon found in the United States. She went on to tend the other owls — the tiny saw-whet owls, the long-eared owls, and the barn owls. She decided to save her visit to the barred owl cage — and the new baby — for later.

Right now, she was scheduled to give a short talk to a group of children from a summer school program. She teamed up with Chip, an educator at the Center. Chip had a peregrine falcon perched on his arm. Hannah and Chip gave the children a chance to watch the peregrine for a while before answering questions.

"Hey, it's got a mustache!" said one girl, giggling.

"My uncle's got a mustache."

"I like its black hood," said another kid.

"Yeah, that's cool."

"Does it eat rabbits and stuff?"

"No, peregrines eat birds," said Hannah. "They're so fast they can catch birds in midair. Falcons are the fastest fliers in the world. When they dive at their prey, it's called "stooping." They can dive at speeds up to 200 miles per hour!"

"Are they endangered?"

"They were almost extinct," said Hannah. "Many years ago, farmers sprayed a chemical called DDT on their crops to get rid of bugs. It was really bad for the environment because it got into the food chain. Bugs that had been sprayed with DDT were eaten by birds, and then

OWL'S AMAZING HEARING

With their incredibly keen hearing, owls can detect sounds at least ten times fainter than humans can. For instance, an owl can hear a mouse stepping on a twig 75 feet away.

Owls have flat, disk-like faces with stiff feathers that help direct every sound to their ear openings. You can't see an owl's ear openings because they're hidden by feathers, but they're often very large — as long as the whole head in some owls. Some species, such as the great horned owl, have feathery "ear tufts," but these are not really ears, just fancy feathers. Some species of owls have one ear that is slightly higher than the other one. This allows them to pinpoint the direction and distance of prey in total darkness with amazing accuracy. Sound coming from above seems slightly louder in the ear with the higher opening, while sound at eye level is equally loud in both ears.

Chip shows off a peregrine falcon to a group of students.

peregrine falcons ate the birds. The DDT weakened the shells of the peregrines' eggs, so the peregrines began to die out."

"Is this bug stuff still being used?"

"Not in the United States," said Hannah. "It was banned in the early 1970s. But it's still around in the environment, and some countries still use it. Even so, the peregrines *are* coming back."

"Was this one messed up by DDT?"

"No," said Hannah, "it hit a window and broke a wing."

The peregrine falcon ruffled its feathers.

"I like the peregrine falcon best!"

After her session with the school group, Hannah finally had a chance to check on the baby barred owl. She moved quietly into the cage and placed three dead mice on a platform beside the adult female and the baby. The adult owl ruffled her brown-gray feathers and watched with big, wide eyes. Hannah stepped out of the cage and waited. The adult grabbed a mouse in her talons and tore off a piece with her beak. She held it out to the young owl. The infant snatched the food.

"All *right!*" said Hannah with satisfaction.

It looked as if the adult owl had adopted the orphan, and the little one was eating well. It was a good sign. If the owlet kept eating and growing, it would lose its downy feathers, and its adult plumage would grow in. By fall, Hannah hoped, it would be ready to fly and hunt on its own.

TOP OF THE FOOD CHAIN

A grasshopper eats grass; a shrew eats the grasshopper; a red-tailed hawk eats the shrew. This is called a food chain, and raptors are up at the top. A top predator is an animal that is not preyed upon by any other animals. Other carnivores, or meat-eaters, that are top predators include lions, alligators, killer whales, and humans.

As top predators, birds of prey are the best mousetraps going. They play an important role in the balance of nature by keeping mice populations under control. This helps humans, too. Can you imagine farmers trying to grow crops with fields full of rodents?

In addition to rodents, raptors eat insects, fish, snakes, frogs, rabbits, and, in the case of falcons, smaller birds. A few large eagles even prey on small deer and antelope. One type of raptor that doesn't catch live prey is the vulture. Vultures act as nature's "clean-up crews," feeding on carrion (the flesh of animals that have already died).

CHAPTER 3

Behind the Scenes

Mike, the director of the Raptor Center, is a trained wildlife biologist.

While visitors to the Vermont Raptor Center are enjoying the birds in the public viewing area, there's always a lot of activity going on behind the scenes to keep the Center running and the birds healthy. After Hannah had finished checking all the raptors on display, it was time for her duties in the private section of the Center.

Outside the infirmary, Hannah met with Mike, the Raptor Center's director, and other volunteers to discuss the afternoon's work. The volunteers were as diverse as the raptors themselves. Sam was studying chemistry at a nearby college. Ted studied art. Hannah loved languages and wildlife, and she hoped someday to work in a field that would combine her interests.

All the volunteers at the Center had received more than 15 weeks of training in handling and rehabilitating raptors and in teaching visitors about the birds. Hannah had grown up loving animals and caring for them. Two years before, when she had first learned about the volunteer program at the Raptor Center, she had known it would be perfect for her. Now she was working about 20 hours a week at the Center.

Though she was considered a senior volunteer, she handled every chore that needed to be done, from cleaning rodent cages to releasing raptors into the wild. In any given week, Hannah might go on a field rescue, as she had that morning, treat a wounded bird, or force-feed a bird that couldn't eat by itself.

On this day, Mike asked Hannah to show Sarah, a new volunteer, how to tend to the rodents in the infirmary building. Hannah met Sarah, and they went down to the basement, where the live mice and rats were kept in metal cages.

"Raising mice and rats is an important part of this job," Hannah told Sarah. "You have to feed them and check their water. We clean the cages about twice a week."

"I've never seen so many mice and rats."

Hannah laughed. "We call it our rodent explosion room. And it's a good thing they keep having more babies. We use the adult rodents in training the young birds to capture live prey before we release them.

Hannah grabbed a rat by the tail and put it in a bucket while she cleaned its cage. The rat was as big as a kitten.

"Eeeew! How did you ever get used to this?"

"I know. I used to think it was gross," said Hannah. "But the cages have to be cleaned, so you just get used to it. The first time is definitely the weirdest."

Hannah held out the rat. "Want to try?" she asked.

"Aaaaaaaah. . . . I guess so."

Sarah took the rat by the tail and held it out at arm's length. The rat began to squirm, and she quickly handed it back to Hannah.

Cleaning rodent cages is all in a day's work for Hannah.

"You're right. That was very weird!"

After showing Sarah how to feed the rodents and clean their cages, Hannah went upstairs to tend the birds in the infirmary. The cages there held birds that needed a lot of attention and care. There was an osprey that had arrived with swollen feet and a bad scrape on its wing. There was a rough-legged hawk with foot sores. And there were kestrel chicks that seemed to need constant feeding.

Hannah went first to help an adult kestrel that needed medicine. She held the bird in one gloved hand and squirted the medicine into its beak with a dropper. Next, she had to feed two abandoned kestrel chicks. She took a dead mouse from the refrigerator and cut it into small pieces with scissors. The first time she cut up a mouse, she thought it was horrible. But now it didn't bother her.

With her gloved hand cradling the downy body of a kestrel chick, Hannah used her other hand to feed the bird. She used tweezers so she could get the mouse chunks close to the kestrel's sharp little beak without getting her fingers pinched. The kestrel took a piece in its beak, closed its eyes, and swallowed.

Hannah fed the kestrel chicks one piece after another. This was one of her favorite parts of her work at the Center. Except for releasing a bird back into the wild, Hannah felt that nothing was as satisfying as watching a young hawk or owl with a big appetite. It was always a good sign that the bird was on the road to full recovery.

Hannah finished with the young patients and went to help Sam, another volunteer, treat the rough-legged hawk's sore feet. Sometimes birds of prey in captivity get sores on their feet. Raptor workers call it

Hannah squirts a dropperful of
medicine into a kestrel's open
beak.

"bumblefoot." The sores are caused by improper perching. In the wild, raptors are constantly moving from one branch to another, and the branches are all different sizes. But in captivity, the birds sometimes perch on the same branch, in one spot, for hours, and that causes pressure sores.

Handling a large adult raptor, such as a hawk, is a two-person job. One person holds the bird and controls the dangerous beak and talons; the other person concentrates on the work at hand. Birds of prey are wild, and raptor volunteers are careful to handle them only when absolutely necessary. Too much handling can cause stress to a wild bird.

While Sam held the hawk, Hannah unwrapped the bandages on one of the bird's feet and examined the foot closely.

"This is looking much better, don't you think?" she asked Sam.

"It's healing really well," said Sam. "This guy could run a race pretty soon."

Sam held on tightly as the hawk struggled and clutched the air with its talons. Hannah removed the rest of the bandages. She spoke softly to the hawk. "Easy, easy now. This will make things better."

Hannah waited until the bird was calm and used a cotton swab to dab the hawk's feet with a soothing medicine. Then she gently reapplied the bandages.

While Sam and Hannah cared for the rough-legged hawk, another volunteer, Ted, and the Center's director, Mike, were tending an osprey, or fish hawk, that had been found by the side of the road. It had an open wound on one of its wing joints, and its feet were badly swollen.

"Have you ever force-fed an osprey?" asked Mike.

"No," answered Ted.

"You're in for a real treat!" Mike chuckled. "Osprey are tough birds to keep in captivity — they usually won't eat by themselves."

While Ted kept a tight hold around the osprey's legs, Mike wrapped a blue cloth around the hawk in preparation for feeding. The osprey looked as if it were at the barber shop, getting ready for a trim.

"I'm going to bare-hand this," Mike said. "The gloves are too clumsy for force-feeding."

Mike grasped the osprey's beak and pried it open with his fingers. Then he grabbed a piece of fish from a plastic tray with a pair of forceps

Hannah dabs some medicine on the foot of a rough-legged hawk.

and quickly but gently forced the food into the osprey's mouth. The osprey swallowed naturally as soon as it felt the fish in its throat. Within minutes, all the small fish in the tray were gone.

After the feeding, the osprey rested in Ted's arms. Fish stains covered the front of its blue "bib."

"You look like a little kid who's just eaten a plate of macaroni," Ted joked.

While Ted returned the osprey to its cage, Mike went to help Heather, another volunteer, update the files on some long-eared owls.

Mike carefully removed one of the owls from its cage with a device

It definitely takes two to force-feed fish to an unwilling osprey.

like a big butterfly net. He scooped the bird out and gently tucked it in the crook of his arm. Then Mike placed a small leather hood over the bird's head to calm it during the examination. He fanned out each wing, feeling the fragile bones. Next, he checked the owl's feathers, talons, and foot pads. Heather noted the owl's condition in the file.

By then it was late afternoon — time for the volunteers on the evening shift to take over. Hannah had finished her chores and was going back to check on the baby barred owl again.

"Hey, Hannah, you going to stay all night?" shouted Sam. He and two other volunteers waved to Hannah on their way out.

"See you guys tomorrow," called Hannah. She grabbed her backpack and took one last look at the young barred owl before she left for the day. On a high perch in a corner of the cage, the owl dozed in the warm afternoon sunshine.

CHAPTER 4

Back to the Wild

Hannah loaded the barred owl she had rescued into the Center's station wagon.

The time had come to free the young barred owl. All summer long, Hannah had watched the bird grow strong and healthy. By fall, it had its adult feathers. After a week of catching live mice in its own cage, the young owl was ready to go back to the wild.

One September morning, Hannah stepped into the young barred owl's cage. She reached out with gloved hands and firmly grasped its legs. She carried the bird outside the cage and put it into a box in the back of the Center's station wagon.

It was an hour's drive to the woods where the owl would be released. On the way, Hannah thought about the morning when she had found the baby owl in the woods, and about the bird's first days at the Center. The little owl had seemed so fragile, huddled there on the forest floor, and so alone without its parents. But with the help of the surrogate mother owl and Hannah, it had adjusted well to its new surroundings. Now she was glad this owl was going back to its natural home.

The car stopped along a wooded stretch of road. Migrating warblers and vireos moved in the upper branches of the trees, their calls sounding

Now a fully feathered adult, the barred owl was ready for release.

BIRD BANDING

Before a raptor is returned to the wild, a small metal band is placed around the bird's lower leg. This band carries a serial number, as well as the address of the Bird Banding Laboratory in Laurel, Maryland. If the bird is ever found dead or is captured, the number on the band can be sent to the Banding Lab, and the bird's history can be traced.

Through banding, ornithologists (people who study birds) learn about migration timing and routes, how long birds live, and why they die. Bird banding began around 1920. Since then, more than 40 million birds have been banded in North America. However, only 5 percent of the birds banded each year are recaptured or recovered.

like faraway bells. Hannah carried the box with the owl up a forested slope. The place was perfect barred-owl country, full of swampy woodlands.

Hannah walked a mile or so from the road, over a ridge, and down into an open section of woods with a small creek running into a shallow pond. Around the clearing stood old maple trees and slender white pines. Hannah set the box down in the middle of the clearing and put on a pair of heavy leather gloves that went halfway up her arms. She

Flung from Hannah's outstretched arm, the owl took wing.

unlatched the box, reached in, and grasped the owl's feathery legs. As she lifted the bird high over her head, the barred owl flapped its wings, testing their strength, anxious to be off.

Hannah held the owl for a few moments and watched it adjust to the forest. The owl rotated its head first one way, then the other, surveying its new surroundings. The large, alert eyes watched almost imperceptible stirrings in the trees and in the leaves on the woodland floor. A soft breeze fanned the bird's thick, light-brown breast feathers.

"Okay, little guy, time to go," Hannah said. She stepped closer to the woods and waved the owl into the air. The bird spread its wings and flew to a narrow branch. It was a clumsy landing. The owl almost tipped over, and it beat its wings to gain a proper footing. "You'll learn," Hannah said softly. Then the barred owl launched itself neatly from the branch and flew silently into the forest.

Hannah watched the owl fly farther and farther into the woods. She followed it a short distance; then it glided slowly among the trees and out of sight. Hannah stood for a moment and looked around. The forest was very still. The only sound was the wind swishing through the tops of the tallest pines. The owl was home.

The owl paused to survey the forest — home at last.

Index